AARON THE AARDVARK
GETS ANTSY

WRITTEN BY
DAVID McKINNEY

ILLUSTRATED BY
HANNAH TUOHY

David McKinney lives in Tulsa, Oklahoma.
He practices law, backpacks, works on
physics problems (really), and comes up
with the worst puns ever.

David has told stories to his children since
1982. Some of them are true.

Aaron the Aardvark, a young boy, is energetic -- and forgetful.
He forgets to clean his lunchbox. When the ants move in,
Aaron has a special treat.

A read-aloud book with poetry, word-plays, and treats both
for the child and the adult reader.

ISBN: 978-0-692-42801-6

For Stephen, Scott, and Amber, for whom
Aaron came to life.

Parents:

Drink some choc'late,
Make a lap;
Read this book
Before a nap.

Calming tones
Are best to read.
Use them well
And plant a seed.

Read to kids --
Your love expressed;
Kids will know
That they are blessed.

Not a parent? Read ahead,
A kid will listen before bed.

Once upon a time there was an aardvark
named Aaron, and he was always getting
into mischief. If you don't know what
"mischief" is, read the last page.

Aaron took his lunch to school. His mom told him: "Be sure to rinse out your lunchbox."

Aaron, however, forgot. He didn't forget one day; he forgot for a whole month.

Aaron's lunchbox started to
smell funny when he opened it.

He didn't care, because his lunch still tasted good. "Phew," said Penelope the Pig. "Blech," said Bob the Bear.

Funny smells smell good to ants.
Pretty soon, ants found their way
to Aaron's lunchbox. One ant
wriggled in through a small crack.

The ant showed other ants how to get in.

When Aaron opened his lunch box, his
food was black with hundreds of ants!

You might not want to eat food that is covered with ants, but aardvarks love ants! That's why they have long, pointy, snouts and longer, sticky, tongues. Aaron had a special treat for lunch!

But from then on, Aaron's mom
packed his lunch in a sack.

Definition

"Mischief" means trouble that you can get into. Sometimes, you can get into mischief just because bad luck happens. Sometimes, you get into mischief because you don't pay attention to your surroundings.

Sometimes, you get into mischief because you act a little wild. Then, people may call you "mischievous."

You may think that Mischief means a single woman who leads an Indian Tribe. She wouldn't be a mischief; she would be a Miss Chief.

Her first name would be Hanker, and she would wipe her runny nose with a white cloth - a handkerchief.

CPSIA information can be obtained at www.ICGtesting.com
Printed in the USA
LVIW01n0155210517
534969LV00003B/5